THE UBER CAT & DRAGON HANDBOOK

A Pet Owner's Guide

Marge Simon and Mary Turzillo

Sam's Dot Publishing

Acknowledgements

Some of the works included in this collection first appeared as follows: "Augmented" in *Your Cat & Other Space Aliens*, Mary Turzillo (vanZeno), 2007, "Dinosaurs May Be Ancestors of More than Birds," Mary Turzillo, *Asimov's SF Magazine*, August 1996, "The Hunter's Mothers" , Mary Turzillo *Asimov's SF Magazine*, March 1998, "A Matter of Conscience", Marge Simon, *Sorcerous Signals*, September 2010, "More Ways to Tell If Your Cat Is a Space Alien", Mary Turzillo, *Asimov's SF Magazine*, April 2001, "Scout," Mary Turzillo, *Cat Tales*, ed. George Scithers, (Wildside), September 2008.

All other work is original to this volume

First Edition

ISBN ???

Sam's Dot Publishing
P.O. Box 782
Cedar Rapids, IA 52406-0782

samsdot@samsdotpublishing.com
www.samsdotpublishing.com/

CONTENTS

THE UBER CAT & DRAGON HANDBOOK

A Pet Owner's Guide

CHOOSING YOUR NEW PET

Your Darling New Dragon

So your kid wants a dragon for his birthday? Not to fret! Hundreds of parents have given the gift that teaches respect for mythology to their kids, and found the whole family rewarded by years, possibly generations, of devotion from a pet that is becoming more and more popular.

We asked Dr. Mary Ann Mantell, D.V.M., author of <u>No Bad Dragon</u>, some questions about dragons as pets. Dr. Mantell herself owns a young Wyvern and a flock of Fire Iguanas. "We started off with just a pair of Fire Iguanas," she laughs, "But you have to remember those guys multiply like mad. At last count, we had nineteen – and Broilerette, our eldest female, looks like she's gravid again. It's loads of fun for my whole family!"

The first question any pet-owner has to ask is, "Why a dragon?" After all, there are lots of homeless kittens and puppies in the world, or, if your taste leans to the exotic, mere-cats, aardvarks, and of course the now trendy Sabertooth Tiger, better known as Smilodons.

Dr. Mantell is very positive on dragon ownership. "These guys need love as much as any other animal. They teach your child responsibility. And some of them are excellent as watch animals or vermin catchers. You can bet we don't have many pesky rats or birds since we acquired our wyvern. And burglars? Forget it!. There was a complaint about a prowler getting eaten, but the police haven't found anything, and we just point out, there is no evidence.

"But you have to be willing to accept responsibility for an animal with special needs. Remember, that cute dragon chick dragging your station wagon around as a pull-toy will very quickly become a playful forty-foot adolescent, with a hearty appetite and a strong instinct for crashing over fences and houses to find a virgin. They do have to be spayed, or they will roam and lay eggs. Ask yourself if your kids will get upset if Mom cooks up Draggy's babies into breakfast for ten!"

So what kind of dragon should you choose for your child?

"A lot depends on the child's personality," said Dr. Mantell. "A strong active child might enjoy the playfulness of a Welsh Red Dragon. But think twice before you invest in a Welshie chick; they aren't for everybody. If you do go for one of the more active reptiles, I suggest one of the smaller ones, perhaps an Imoogi. Believe me, the neighbors will be just as impressed!"

Dr. Mantell fails to mention that Imoogi grow to be huge, ferocious man-eaters as adults. Of course, since it takes them over a thousand years to attain full size, this is a problem you can ignore for the present. Watch out for the safety of your descendents, though!

A shyer child may prefer a cuddly Komodo, with its adorable waddle, according to Mantell. These are readily available, but be warned they are not recognized as officially mythological. They have to be fenced in carefully, of course, and fitted early in childhood with a muzzle, as their bite is quite poisonous.

Then there are the Fur-bats. They tend to be one-person pets, but less aggressive. These plant-eaters are only a problem if you're a stickler for fancy landscaping. Any plant-eating dragon will graze your property clean, and a Fur-bat is not a critter I'd advise for any but the most dedicated pet-owner.

We asked Dr. Mantell if a Flame-Tipped-George-Muncher might be a good pet. "Too high-strung for young children," she advises. "A patient adult who knows how to fend off those love-nips might enjoy a Georgie, though."

How about Neon Thousand-Wing? "They tend to fly off. You can cage them, but what's the point? A pet is to love, not to imprison."

Are there dragon pets for apartment-dwellers? "Try a Dracomussie. They're only eight inches long as adults, and they breed like rabbits."

– *Mary Turzillo*

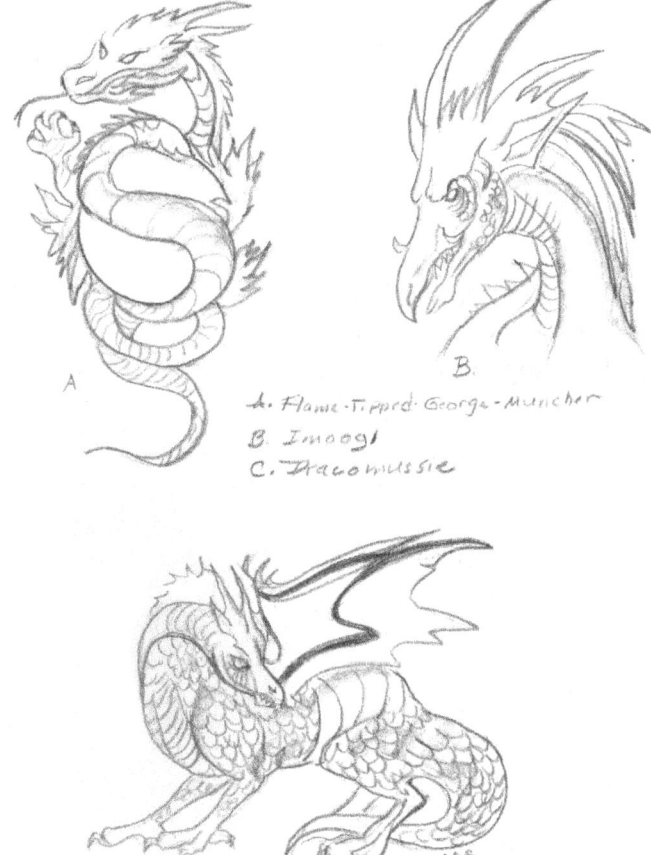

A.

B.

A. Flame-Tipped George-Muncher
B. Imoogi
C. Dracomussie

C.

The Dragon in the Window

How much is that dragon in the window?
The one with the straggly green tail,
How much is that dragon in the window?
I do hope that dragon's for sale.

I must take a trip to New Jersey,
And leave my poor sweetheart alone,
With a dragon, he won't be lonesome,
And the dragon will have a good home.

(chorus)

In his town there are nasty robbers,
With flashlights, for they're all the same,
My love needs a dragon to protect him,
And scare them with one burst of flame.

I don't want a pet rock or bunny,
I don't want a parrot that talks,
I don't want a bowl of little fishies
He can't take a goldfish for walks.

(chorus)

I can't afford a new web cam,
Can't give him the latest cell phone,
A dragon will stave off his lonesome,
And the dragon will have a good home.

This song is so very simplistic
It's driving me nuts just to sing,
But a dragon has so many talents,
You can train it to do anything.

(ANYTHING? I WANT ONE!)

How much is that dragon in the window?
The one with the straggly green tail,
How much is that dragon in the window?
I do hope that dragon's for sale.

– Marge Simon

Little Serpent Girl

(sung by the Bleach Boys)

Little dragon little one
Made my heart come all undone
Do you love me
do you dragon girl
Serpent girl my little wyrmoid girl

I have watched you on the shore
Standing by the ocean's roar
Do you love me do you dragon girl
serpent girl wyrmoid girl

We could ride the surf together
While our love would grow
In my hoody I would take you everywhere I go
So I say from me to you
I will make your dreams come true
Do you love me do you dragon girl
Serpent girl my little wyrmoid girl

Well
Girl dragon girl my little dragon girl
Well
Girl dragon girl my little dragon girl
Well
Girl dragon girl my little dragon girl

– Marge Simon

Selecting the Perfect Uber Cat

Experts agree that this is a difficult undertaking, but once you have made the right choice, your life will be changed radically, hopefully for the better. If your children survive the first few days, they will be ever thankful. Studies have shown that timid girls and wimpy boys make the best choices for uber cat owners. If you are childless or single, you have more of a variety to consider.

Phantom Cats - Possibly the cleanest of uber felines, these make perfect cats for apartment living. Not known to cause allergies in humans. Although they are loveable kittens, they may become rather hard to see on maturing. Small children can see them just fine, but if you have company in for a wine tasting, it's advisable to spell them into another area of the surrounds.

Spells for phantom cats can be found in _The Book of Phantom Spells for Cats_ by Horatio Pulsar, Stein & Sons, London, 1867. Not currently available on Amazon.com. Try an old bookstore on a dark, dirty street in the rustic section of a vast city.

Oriental Ubers -You'll adore your baby Persian Faust. Kittens retain their fluffy cuteness for centuries before turning against their owners. At that time, it's advisable to leave.

Tokyo Rosers - a silky ebon longhair, these make fine pets for the faint of heart. For about five minutes. Their yowl can shatter glass.

Russian Ubers - The Minsk Blue Devil makes a good companion for those who love the outdoor wilderness.

Camping trips may include wolverine sports.

For those who prefer less active breeds, the Leningrad Lurker may be for you.

Owner's testimonial (translated):

"The Lurker is in fact a true psychopath. Even more baffling than other uber breeds. She gets on top of us and holds us down against our will, sometimes for hours, despite the fact that she weighs less than six pounds. Last night she decided she wanted to sleep with her paw covering my mouth and nose. Every time I tried to get away, she planted her paw firmly blocking my air path. I finally gave up and tried to get a meager amount of oxygen through her fur.

She is the cat that put my husband in the hospital twice. The vet pretends not to be afraid of her, but I know she is. But our baby's main weapon is the hypnotic purr. If she didn't have to get up and use the litter box periodically, we'd be dead husks." - Mrs. Anya Nabakovia

Para - according to legends, ancient Finnish household spirits who appear in the shape of a cat. They enlarge to amount of food and money with what they stole elsewhere. Don't be fooled. The Para is no legendary cat. It resembles the Persian, with a long, silky coat and snub nose. Do not attempt grooming. Its hair is capable of constricting and has been known to strangle fishwives, postmen, and passersby. If you are unsure whether you have a Para or a Persian, ask a Gyspy. Should your Para become uncommonly large, contact the authors of this book.

Stratavari - Multicolored, as in calico or tortoise shell. Do not feed at night. Open the windows. The Stratavari's hidden skin flaps unfold to a wingspan of seven to ten feet. It's a marvelous sight to see a cat soar. The Stratavari will share its kill with you if you have been taking proper care of it. Tasmanian Rex - Found deep in the thick junk piles of Tasmania, the T-Rex hails from an ancient lineage of scrappers, thought to be left behind by early alien visitors. Accidentally on purpose, most likely. These mighty beasts weigh up to 568.7 pounds. Generally known for a bad disposition, but if you are lucky enough to raise it from birth, you might enjoy its unique company. Properly trained, the Rex makes a faithful watch-cat, particularly if you don't like human company.

Grimalkin - Gray cat of Celtic heritage with magical powers. Familiar to witches. Grimalkins tend to be short hairs, with a coat of steely gray and green eyes. Easily spotted by the pointy sharp thing on the end of its tail, used for starting fires. Size varies: 4 x 4 inches is normal, but some have been reported as large as 24 feet long. Warning: Eye color changes from green to puce when communicating with Satan.

Nostradamus had a familiar by this name, so it may well have been of the same breed. Fabled as an "evil looking cat", the true Scottish Grim is bears up to this description, mostly associated with females of the breed. Males may appear skittish, with complicated personalities. The female is very low maintenance, perfect company for the writer or poet. Often associated with witchcraft, a Grim would be a good choice for a horror fan. Serious necromancers need to check out a full pedigree before purchase. The cost may be high, but the rewards are excellent.

Common Hallowe'en Disappearing Black Cat - (similar to the Phantom Cat, but unfortunately tend to manifest at inconvenient times, as when your allergic nephew plops down on the sofa for a cookie and a glass of milk). If you're superstitious, this breed is not the best choice.

Smilodon (Sabertooth) - These majestic felines weigh up to a ton. They make excellent guardians, having a natural instinct to protect their territory. Adoption waiting lists are extremely long, so get your name on the list as soon as possible.

Characteristics: fourteen inch incisors (thus, their fanciful name); playful when not on duty. Toys: sheep, gazelles, rejects from American Idol and aging Survivor stars.

Miniature Smilodon (Miniature Sabertooth) - a much smaller, trendy version, these sweet natured ubers are best matched in homes of problem teenagers. You will be able to take vacations and leave your kids at home. Mini-Smilodons are allergic to smoke, drugs, alcohol and loud noise. If exposed to such, their sweet nature evaporates in a wink.

Mercat - According to legend, this Scottish breed was first spotted sunning itself on the banks of Loch Ness. If your family enjoys water sports, a Mercat is for you.

Furwing - of common alley cat extraction, this mutant British breed makes an excellent companion for all ages. Not recommended for bird lovers. As soon as they are weaned, they can take to the air with few mishaps. If you must display those silly "Precious Moments" statuettes, put them in a glass cabinet.

Furwings do particularly well in high altitudes such as Chile, Colorado, and the Alps and enjoy family vacations to such areas. Hearty indoor/outdoor cats, they do not do well cooped up inside. A kitty door is a must.

–Dr. Phillipia Albright, Feline Specialist, U.C.S

– *Marge Simon*

A. Puma
B. Smilodon
C. Grimalkin

A.

B.

C.

19

More Ways to Tell If Your Cat Is a Space Alien

1. Your cat came from a pet store in Roswell, New Mexico.

2. You find long distance charges on your telephone bill to area codes the operator has never heard of.

3. You come home to find your cat walking on the ceiling, and your cat just looks at you and says, "Yeah, so?"

4. Your cat goes hunting and brings you home a Little Green Mouse.

5. Your cat's eyes glow in the dark. Even when they're closed.

6. When you scratch your cat behind the ears, you notice she has antennae.

7. Your cat volunteers to remove your brain.

8. You agree to have your cat remove your brain.

9. Your cat can program your computer better than you can.

10. Your cat can program your computer better than your ten-year-old kid can.

11. You discover that your cat has a glitzier Web page than you do.

12. You discover your cat has put you up for adoption on the Internet.

13. UPS arrives at your front door with a cage to take you to your new owner – on 51 Pegasi Prime.

– *Mary Turzillo*

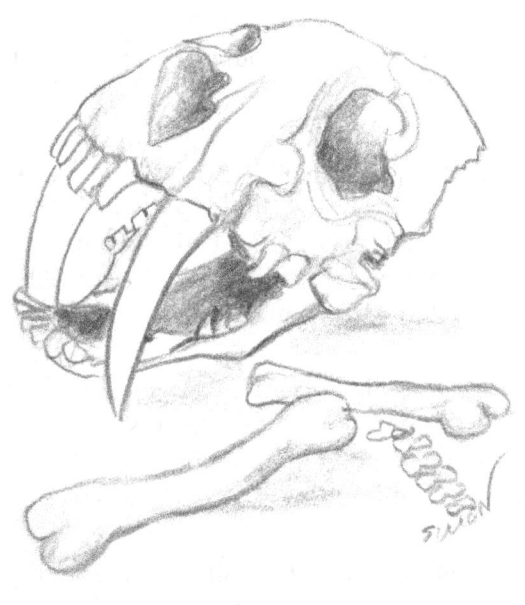

ANCESTORS

Dinosaurs May Not Be Ancestors of Reptiles

Cambridge, 2011: Wormologist Dr. Suzi Silverscale's recent paper on dragon ancestry opens new avenues of speculation. "The extremely obvious is not always factual," she says. "We assumed that dragons began as serpents, but there is now evidence that the opposite is the case. Dragons were around in the Carboniferous period."

First specimen: <u>Slimohederotus</u>, The Wyrm of Pilsar's remains were discovered approximately yesterday in the Sudan. Most assuredly limbless, this 200 foot giant possessed a fully developed brain, long before the first snakes evolved. Whether dragon or snake played a role in the Garden of Eden is for grabs.

Second: The Chinese Five Claw, <u>Notikinowashus,</u> had an enormous feet and a small cranium. Dr. Silverscale surmises that it lived in mountainous areas and probably ate anything it could ingest. Pebbles and crayons were found in its stomach cavity.

Third: The Hydra, present in Greek mythos, was actually the <u>Maniheaddus,</u> whose remains were discovered deep in floor of the Mediterranean.

Fourth: <u>Monthrafoteaus</u>, most certainly the longest tailed dragon in history, haunted the shores of what later became Cincinnati. Its bones proved too delicate for transport, so it exists only in photographs.

Fifth: Dilapator once roamed the area we now call Minsk. His massive hind legs and undeveloped wings assured he was a land dragon. Some believe he may have been around as early as the trilobite.

Sixth: Montezumus stalatyl, believed the first of the frost dragons. Bone fragments and partial skeletons have been found all over South America. The largest specimen with a wingspan of fifteen meters was unearthed in Chile, 2007.

– Marge Simon

Dinosaurs May Be Ancestors of More Than Birds

Paleontologist Dr. Felix Stalker today unveiled three specimens thought to prey on ancestors of birds. "Logic says," according to Stalker, "where there's birds, there's got to be cats."

First specimen: *Acatasaurus*. Originally thought vegetarian, this long-necked ancestor of the Siamese probably fed on prehistoric fish. Early aquariums may be discovered on future digs.

Second: Velocimouser. This quick-witted swift catosaur captured prey by silent stalking, then pouncing. Clever and voracious, it may have gone extinct because caught off guard taking naps after dismembering small mammals.

Most controversial specimens: *Purranosaurus Rex.* Note long, rapacious teeth. Also called Thunder Catosaur because of low rumbling sound emitted after devouring prey or shredding furniture. Small front limbs may not have been as useless as they look.

Dr. Stalker showed bone fragments of other catosaurs "too early to categorize," he said." But tentatively named *Triwhiskerops* (note pointed structures either side its head), *Meowasaurus,* good mother catosaur, *Prrtadactyl, Kittycoatlus,* and *Architsbackterix,* evolutionary blind alleys nature abandoned when catosaurs found they could not leap forty feet. And finally the ancestor of the domestic feline: *Ankylorubbosaur.*

Dr. Stalker plans next summer to seek fossils of a species believed to prey on catosaurs: the *Fidonychus.*

– Mary Turzillo

Invisible Cat

He's invisible
phantasmagorical
ectoplasmical
half-draconical
he's all that
invisible cat.

that litter was extraordinary
Mama cat-eyes distinguished more
Counting kittens, she saw five
but when we looked, we saw just four.
Phantom feline lives with you
He eats your food, he haunts your flat
You saw him as a kitten, how 'bout that?
But now he's vanished: invisible cat.
He leaves a present on the stair
broken feathers, severed paws,
spots of blood or clumps of hair
But when you scream and ask him *what?*
Phantom feline isn't there.

He's invisible
phantasmagorical
ectoplasmical
half-draconical
he's all that
invisible cat

Far from ordinary
cause he suddenly appears
gives you a coronary
first his whiskers then his ears
just as quick he disappears.
Rumors of his hijinks here and there
a mousie squeak, or doggy bark
Someone saw him slinking through the park

26

He's a phantom, he's a ghost
he only comes out in the dark
In your sleep you feel his weight
He settles on your feet or chest
won't let you move, won't let you rest
He's there, in darkness all night long,
but turn the light on, and he's gone!

He's invisible
phantasmagorical
ectoplasmical
half-draconical
he's all that
invisible cat

– *Mary Turzillo*

Scout

Spring equinox. Whirring sound. Flashing lights. Whoosh of advanced propulsion system.

"Mao! Mao! Mao! Mao! Mao! Mao! Mao!"

Door opens. "Scat! Get away from here! Go home!"

"Mao!"

Fifteen minutes elapse.

"Mao! Mao! Mao! Mao! Mao! Mao! Mao! Mao-ao-ao-ao!"

"I told you, scat! Nothing for you here! Go home!"

"Mao! Mao!"

"Go chase some mice. Or birds. I hate birds."

"Maomaomaomao-ao-ao-ao!"

Splash. "There! Does *that* convince you? Now if I can just get back to sleep."

Six hours elapse.

"What? You still here? Somebody dropped you, right? Threw you out of a car? Do you have a collar?"

"Yooooow! Ssssssss! Raaaaawooo!"

"Ow! Forget it. Just be gone when I get home from work."

"Prrt."

Nine hours elapse. Car pulls up, door slams. Footsteps.

"Gone. Thank God. I was scared somebody took me for the cat lady over on Prospect."

Six hours elapse. Door opens.

"Mao?"

"Go away! I'm calling the Animal Warden and that's it. Hear me? Smoked kitty. Nice cyanide gas. Get! Scat!"

"Mao?"

"What are you doing? That has maggots on it. You can't eat that!"

"Prrrrrr."

"You're eating maggoty ham, and purring? That's disgusting!"

"Prrrrrrrrrrr."

"How could anything get hungry enough to eat rotten meat? Wait a minute."

Door closes, opens again.

"Here, here's the rest of my chicken wings. Hope you like garlic honey sauce. They're cold, anyway."

28

"Purrrrrrrrrrrrrrrrrrrr."
"Get away from my legs! I hate that. Didn't I tell you I hate cats?"
Door slams. Eight hours elapse.
"Thank God it's gone. Found some other sucker."
Car door slams. Car starts, zooms away.
Three days elapse.
"Mao, mao, mao, mao, mao, mao, mao."
"You again? I don't have any more chicken wings. And I don't
believe you if you say you're lost, because you left here Friday and
then came back."
"Prrt?"
"Let me look at your collar. I bet some nice little stupid girl is just
weeping her eyes out over you. Woosy woosy woosy woosy."
A brief chase.
"MAO!"
"Okay, so you have a collar, but no name on it. Real stupid little
girl. She deserves to lose a prize flea-bag like you."
"Prrt."
"At least you didn't scratch me again."
Six hours elapse. Dusk gives way to nightfall. The air chills.
"Mao? Mao? Mao? Mao? Mao? Mao? MAO? MAO?
MAOMAOMAOMAO?"
A window opens.
"Shut up down there! Remember what I did the last time you woke
me up?"
Footsteps on stairs. Door opens.
"MAOMAOMAOMAOMAOMAOMAO!"
"Let me guess. You're cold, right? If I give you something to sleep
on, you'll get cat hair all over it. And fleas. And worms. I bet you
have worms, eating garbage like that."
*Door closes. Footsteps, sounds of rummaging. A piece of torn, dirty
carpeting falls out of an upper window, THUMPS on the ground,
raises billows of dust.*
"Mao!"
Silence.
Seven hours elapse.
Door opens. "Where are you? Did you spend the night under the
rug? Great, now what do I do with this piece of shit? I suppose I

have to leave it, in case it's cold again tonight. A decorator touch for my entry."

Car door opens, closes, car speeds away.

Nine hours elapse.

"Here. For your majesty. It was cheap, and it looks better than that rug."

"Mao. Prrt."

"That's right. Show some gratitude, you little rat. You look like a rat, did you know that? You aren't much bigger than a rat. Well, hey, that's what eating maggoty garbage does for you. Not exactly the breakfast of champions. I suppose if I give you a little milk you'll think you can move in here, right? So I won't."

"Mao?"

"Not a chance. Go find your supper somewhere else."

"Mao? Mao?"

"And stop rubbing cat hair all over my pants!"

Door closes. Fifteen minutes elapse.

"Here! Will that shut you up?"

"Prrrrrrrrrrr. Slup. Slup. Slup. Prrrrrr. Slup slup slup slup slup slup slup."

"That's the last you get out of me. I probably don't have enough left for my cereal in the morning."

Twenty four hours elapse.

"Okay, one more time. But I looked up the Animal Shelter on the web. It says they let you stay five days, and then it's curtains for kitty cat. Okay? So I think you should move on."

Four hours elapse.

"Mao! Mao! Mao! Mao!"

"Look I don't have any chicken wings. How about some – french toast? Look, it's good, it's only been in the garbage since yesterday. Eat it. Eat it, you flea bag! It was good enough for me. Are you saying it's not good enough for you? Here, I'll butter it for you. Oh, you like that. Lick the butter off, huh?"

"Mao."

"No! I will not put more butter on it! Eat the whole thing, bread and all."

Twenty four hours elapse.

"Mao! Mao! Mao! Mao!"

30

"Why are you still crying? Didn't you want the french toast? Yich! It's got flies on it."

"Waka."

"Waka? What does that mean? Cats don't say 'waka.' I'm not going to feed you if you don't speak proper English."

"Prrt."

"Wait a minute."

Car door slams. Car takes off. Twenty minutes elapse. Car pulls up. Car door slams.

"Okay, you win. Cat food. This is probably a big mistake, but I'm not going out and buying you chicken wings."

Twelve hours elapse.

"Mao! Mao! Mao! Mao!"

Footsteps stumble down stairs. Door opens.

"At three A.M. you think I'm going to feed you? Oh. Your water overturned on the cat bed. Shit. Here. Here's an old sweatshirt."

"Prrt."

Four hours elapse.

"Here. You didn't ask for it, but I suppose you will. Here's your damn cat food. It stinks. I hope you love it."

"Mao."

"Is that your name, cat? Mao? Like Mao Tse Tung? You don't look Chinese to me." (*Subject kritches cat behind ears.*) "You look – hungry. You're kind of silky – "

A succession of days in which cat food appears in margarine tub. Spring advances. Warm weather. Cat eats food. Subject puts out more cat food.

"Pretty eyes. You might clean up nice. I'd let you in the house, but you'd bring in fleas. Let me think about this."

Subject switches to more expensive brand of cat food.

"You don't want to come in? Last chance."

Autumnal equinox. Whirring sound. Flashing lights. Whoosh of advanced propulsion system.

"Hey, cat! Cat! You didn't eat your food. I'm not going to buy any more unless you eat this. Hey, cat! Hey, Mao! Sneaky-paws! Where are you?"

Door left hopefully ajar.

Twelve hours elapse.

31

"Where are you? Pretty kitty! Mao!"
Another twelve hours.
"Where the hell are you? Mao! Mao! Maaa -oh! Mao! Mao! Mao! Mao!"

– *Mary Turzillo*

The Hunter's Mothers

My new mother gave me milk in a bowl,
groomed me with her large smooth paws,
held me, not in her mouth like my first mother,
but in her big lap, where I fell asleep.

I watched her each day, carefully,
so she could teach me to groom,
and hunt, and mate, and do whatever
was catly for me to perform.

She cut meat that she had caught
somewhere, and put it on plates as big as me
for her other kittens, the large bald ones.
But she never let me have the knife

nor let me play with the meat. Was I unworthy?
I went to the door, thinking she would take me
out in the grass and teach me to hunt.
But she said no.

And when I did go out, she stayed inside
and taught me nothing of hunting.
Perhaps I was too small, my claws too blunt
to catch meat for her and her unfurry kittens.

With practice, I caught a small meaty thing
that wriggled until I batted it to stillness.
Rather than eat it at once, I took it to Mother.
She screamed and threw it away.

Was it not large enough?
Was it not good meat?
I could not get it out of the big can where she puts
uninteresting vegetables and bones.

Later I caught others, but never one she liked much

So I ate them myself, including
the ones that could fly, which I knew
Mother especially did not like.

I have lived a long time with Mother
Her two-legged kittens grew up big, and ran away.
She grooms me when I sit on her lap
but does not thank me for what I catch.

I know I am an unworthy hunter
but how could I learn, when she never taught me?
Maybe she knew I was not as clever as the big meat
that she catches to put on the high table.

So I sleep in a patch of sun
and dream of my first mother,
who went away, but first taught me
I have claws.

– *Mary Turzillo*

Matter of Conscience

"A familiar is a cat by nature"
-Almanac of the Occult

Tallow from the candle had thickened at its base over the past three hours. The ink on the parchment before Lord Gregory had dried and awaited only his signature to be complete. He rubbed a hand over his face several times and blinked his watery eyes in an effort to stay awake.

A large iron gray cat pawed back the drapes and entered the room. It stopped to lick its shoulder, then gave a subdued yowl before leaping to the table.

"So, you've come. I've been expecting you," Gregory said. He scratched the tom's broad head. "Well? What shall I do now, Nim?"

Simple, milord. Sign it.

"Simple? Come now, cat! Nothing is simple about this – not a damned thing.

You're confused. You are thinking too much. It is a task easy enough for you.

"But the fate of my wife is at stake! With the flourish of my quill, I can send her to be tried and convicted as a thief. Lady Sarah would never be spared."

Yet you have an alternative...

"Yes...the alternative. My personal confession to condemning souls under my protection to certain death."

The tradesmen only needed lackeys and whores in return for their pelts—surely not an immediate nor particularly terrible fate for them, all considered.

"Still, I cannot countenance this abomination! Besides, it is forbidden to sell them – "

Be of reasonable mind, milord. I know what has transpired. Consider it a matter of population control. I've had to remove more than one who presumed to share my plate.

"But this was an error, a misunderstanding – "

The cat's whiskers twitched. *It was no error. Your Sarah signed the papers. It was she who sold your own serfs to the barbarian traders – ten of them, correct?*

"Don't remind me," Gregory moaned. His lovely young wife had forged his signature on the sale of seven men and three women to the foreigners in exchange for ermine pelts – enough to make a splendid cape, suitable for royalty. These unfortunates had been listed as debtors outstanding to the King at the last tax collection. Thus, his Majesty's accountants had only recently discovered that they no longer belonged to him. It was a most embarrassing and dangerous state of affairs – one that he had been requested to address immediately. And the King was not known for forbearance when it came to the shady dealings of a minor lord. "If you take anything from your serf over and above taxes to which you are entitled, you do so at the peril of your soul" but the present Crown had further decreed that "lords shall not be allowed to buy or sell their chattel, for they are property of the Royal State.

The robe was for you, was it not? You've not worn it – did it not please you?

"Yes, it's very fine indeed." Gregory felt a flush spread from his neck to his face. "I don't want to talk about it," he scowled.

"My dearest, may I enter?" Lady Sarah's lilting voice suddenly interrupted. Gregory assented quickly, glad for a distraction. "I heard you talking," Sarah said as she breezed in carrying a tray of meat, goat cheese and fruit. Under her arm was a small jug of mead. "Who were you speaking to?" she asked, placing the tray down on the table.

"Eh? Oh, I was just muttering aloud to myself. This is most thoughtful of you, my love."

Sarah busied herself laying out the modest repast. She finished by filling his goblet with the mead. The cat stood up expectantly and she leaned to fondle his ears. "Don't worry, dear old Nim, I've something for you as well."

She brought a napkin from the pocket of her skirts and laid its contents on the stone floor. The cat jumped down to sniff the morsels of raw chicken and satisfied, began to eat. His purr filled the small chamber. Before sampling the food, Gregory hastily placed another piece of parchment to cover the document he'd been deliberating over for hours. Sarah was not to know of this – not yet, at least. Let her think he was working on a request for more farmland. He stopped eating to look up and force a smile in response to her beaming face.

"So, Milord. You won't be much longer up here in this droughty room, will you?"

"I expect not, Sarah. I promise I'll not be more than another hour."

Sarah hesitated at the doorway. "Are you sure you won't be needing me for anything else? How is your poor wrist?" She nodded toward the parchments which he'd put back in front of him.

"Well, – " Gregory began, but she interrupted him, taking a step back from the doorway.

"By chance, I was speaking with Lady Odella of Graywater only recently and she requested I convey her wishes for your speedy recovery. I'd told her how you'd injured your wrist in a hunting accident, and – "

"Sarah!" Gregory said sharply. "My wrist is well enough. As you see, I no longer need the sling. Moreover, you had no business discussing my health with anyone outside of our chambers. My accident was a private matter you should have kept to yourself!"

"Oh, Milord – " Sarah's blue eyes widened in concern. "I do apologize for my ignorance of your sentiments concerning your temporary infirmity! Had I known, I'd never have mentioned how you'd had me to sign your name to that request for land a fortnight past to Lady Odella–

"You *what?!* You foolish woman!" Gregory's tone grew harsh. "What did she say?"

"Only that it was rather peculiar. She said that a mark by your own hand and seal is considered sufficient and that her husband would never trouble her for such requests. We didn't dwell on this, as we were discussing fabrics. But I've upset you, my dear husband. Please forgive my outspokenness."

Gregory took her hand in his and kissed it. "Of course I forgive you, my darling Sarah. Now, no more of this. I must return to – ah, the affairs at hand." Sarah nodded and left him alone without further comment.

My, my. Aren't you the solicitous husband! Nim was again perched on the tabletop.

"You know why I did it, Nim."

And she never suspected a thing, signing the document for you. Forging your name at your own request – like a dutiful wife. Nim's eyes were black whirlpools flooding his head.

"I had my reasons, at the time. I didn't think they'd bother with ten missing – I was planning to tell them that the debtors had fled. But I couldn't manage that, when they questioned me."

You can't pretend to me, you know I don't care anything about your excuses. You'd intended all along to put this on Sarah if something went amiss. You knew the signature would appear forged to the eyes of the Royal Assessors – a fact that would serve you well as proof of your own innocence. She is expendable, just like the woman who preceded her as your Lady of the Estate. But you had planned on that one, didn't you? The cat's tail twitched.

"She was hardly comely in the first place – nothing like Sarah. Besides, it was an arranged marriage. Was it my fault that she choked on a bone from the partridge?"

She died by your hands on her throat, to be precise.

Gregory swore an oath, almost knocking over the candle with his arm. "Enough! you are my witness! My confidant! Stop plaguing me with accusations – "

I accuse you of nothing. I am stating facts.

Gregory toyed with the blank parchment. Finally, he laid it beside the other by the candle. "What would you have me do, Nim? On one is my account of Lady Sarah's misdeeds confessing I knew nothing of her devious scheme. On the other – ?" He raised a questioning eyebrow to the cat.

You know you need only to appear to make a choice. If you consider yourself so honorable, then write your own confession on the second sheet – you must at least make this a decision between two documents instead of vaporous excuses.

Gregory wiped his eyes. "Sarah is the finest wife any man could want. I owe her this, you are right." He took up the quill and wrote a second confession, leaving out mention of anyone but himself.

Sign it.

Gregory inked the quill and hastily signed his name. "But more than this I cannot do alone – you choose for me, Nim." The cat stood and padded forward, stopping on top of a paper.

You're not feeling well, are you?

"No," he admitted. In fact, he had been feeling strangely since drinking the mead. Perhaps the beverage had enhanced his fatigue. He had an urgent need to lie down and sleep.

I'm sitting on the one you expected me to chose. Now, affix your seal – use the candle, the stamp..that's fine, we're done!

His perception had become increasingly blurred and everything on the table appeared to spin about in circles. Gregory tried to hold up his head which felt very heavy as he did what Nim had bidden. Then he slumped heavily back into his chair and the stamp slipped from his limp fingers. Five seconds later he was snoring loudly, chin resting on his chest.

The cat snatched the paper barely as the ink dried and darted with it in his mouth out through the doorway where Sarah was waiting in the hall.

Here, take this. His seal is on the one he was so sure I'd choose. Foolish dolt! He will sleep from the drug you gave him for many hours – enough time to have the guards back here before he wakes. I'm sure I can dispose properly of the other version in the hearth – a healthy flame burns in the grate?

"Yes, I've kept it fed myself. I don't know how to thank you, Nim – I still don't understand why you revealed yourself to me. But now, the servants are in quarters – should I – ?"

No. You won't need assistance. Lady Odella's carriage should be arriving any minute. She'll take you to the Sheriff and put you up until it is appropriate for your return to the Manor. Do not thank me. Lady Odella's fine tabby would interest me more than your ministrations.

"But why – ?"

Lord Gregory is a short-sighted fool, blinded by avarice. He once tried dabbling with incantations for a lark, and I was the result. When he realized I could talk to him and no one else could hear us, he became so distraught – it was most disgusting. I gave him to think I'd be his spirit guide – a consolation to his conscience and he'd accepted this idea most eagerly.

"I have heard of spirits – nefarious entities, used by witches to cause trouble of Unholy nature. Yet you speak to me and you do not seem so!" Lady Sarah exclaimed.

If you mean to imply that I cannot be a wicked spirit as I have done you a good, why do you not question my obedience to your Lordship? I'll save your asking. You see, your husband's conjure was incomplete and further complicated than it would have been in skilled hands. I was bidden to the material world to take possession of Nim. Unfortunately, due to his bumbling I am constrained to occupy this body for the time being. Yet there is a fortune to it as well, for I need no longer remain in company with the fool who summoned me. Until I find someone skilled in the arts of Darkness, I remain as you behold.

"Very well. I shall not take vain credit for your help," she said. When he returned from the chamber a second time bearing the other document for disposal, she hurried to question him yet again."Wait, Nim! I'm most curious about one other thing..."

The cat paused, halfway to the staircase. *What would that be, Lady Sarah?*

"Surely you know what I am thinking, Nim!" she chided.

You are wondering what interest I – a creature of the spirit world – would have in Lady Odella's tabby! It is a matter certainly no business of yours – but I will allow that you have earned a right to my secret. in this Nim-body I may enjoy certain pleasures. Instinctual and base, you would say – of too gross a nature to be specific in the presence of your Ladyship.

"Is Lady Odella's female in season?" Sarah addressed Nim's disappearing shadow.

I'll be calling around..

And she knew he'd be back. He was, after all, a cat.

– Marge Simon

41

Hole in the Sky

My father was the first to discover the hole in the sky. He was outside planting glass. It was out of season for blue glass, but he didn't care.

"It sounded like a broken zipper," he said. "Then this hole appeared." The news spread quickly. Everyone came out to admire the hole. It was decided to name it after my father. So it was Sebastian's Hole. My father was given the key to the town and a certificate. The mayor held a big ceremony. There were fireworks and a parade. But after we'd settled down from all the celebrating, we had problems.

Small cats with women's faces began to fall through the hole. My father, now the expert, concluded they came from a parallel universe. We couldn't do anything about it. They were here to stay. First we put them in cages. But they cried too much, their little claws gripping the bars. We talked about adopting them out as pets, but nobody was very excited about it.

We were getting so many of them, we finally decided to put them on display in wire baskets. It had become quite a tourist attraction. Guests were encouraged to feed them raw liver. When visiting hours were over, we sprayed the little tykes with rosewater.

An unforeseen event followed shortly after we'd gotten things under control. A second hole appeared, releasing scores of flying lizards. Crone Mahti said they were dragons. She is so old, she can remember everything since history began. So she's probably right. We captured them and put them into cages too. They smelled like burnt onions. Rosewater didn't help.

My father, who was a Big Name now, suggested someone could try plugging up the holes. A neighbor said he'd provide a ladder, but he had a bad back. Nobody wanted to climb up that high. I'd do it myself if I weren't a writer.

– *Marge Simon*

BRAIN AUGMENTATION

Augmented

Cat sez
whut tukya so long, I wuz hungry.
I sez
lemme get inna door, will ya? You ain't even dunna dishes.
Cat sez
I don't like ta get wet, the suds don't taste good.
I sez, huh.
ya can't even ansa the phone.
I musta rung ten times. Ya cudda toined the crockpot on.
Goddam cat. Goddam whiny cat.
She stretches, sez
that's the breaks. Ja bring me some livah?
LIVAH!? I sez.
Yuh can't even toin on the goddam crockpot.
LIVAH? I atta put you back on cat chow.
Ain't even paid me back for your
Augmentation Operation.
Huh, she sez. Big deal.
Experiment on innocent felines.
Yeah, I sez. Shudda gotcha spayed instead.
Wyncha getta job? Ya so goddam smart now.
What? asks the cat. Operate a computer keyboard
with these teeny tiny paws?
Yeah, I sez. What, ya think they'd hire you on tv, like Robocat?
Ya too ugly, with that lop ear, I sez.
Cats can't get jobs, she sez. 'Sagainst the child labor laws.
I'm only three years old.
Too bad ya too ugly to peddle ya tail onna street, I sez.It's all ya
good for.
More'n you are, she sez.
Sets in ta licking her front paws, in between the toes.
I lose it. Goddam cat.
Here, I sez,
take the rest of this stinkin tunafish and shove it.

And while ya at it, I sez, get out and don't come back.
She looks at me, insolent like.
Wraps her tail around her.
'Sokay, she sez.
I'm booking.
Send me my mail, I'll send a man around in the morning for my
stuff.
And I'm looking at an empty door frame.
Jeez.
Round Christmas, I hear she's moved to Soho.
Part of a dance act.
Adagio dancing, or maybe it's krumping.
Word is, she's suing me.
Suing
ME – for Wrongful Intelligence.

– *Mary Turzillo*

Lady Gaga's Uber Cat

Don't call me Gaga
That cat is a monster
That cat is a monster
it ate my heart
ate, ate, ate

Don't talk no more,
My pet is a monster
My pet is a monster
it yowls at me
yowls, yowls yowls

Don't you touch me
I'm pretty crazy
I'm now the monster
shriek, shriek, shriek.

– *Marge Simon*

EXERCISE

Exercising your Dragon: depends on the breed; flying dragons must be allowed to fly on migrations or during TV commericals. Most other breeds prefer to eat and sleep once reaching maturity, and providing all their many, many special needs are satisfied.

Exercising your Uber Cat: not needed.

– Marge Simon

GROOMING

Uber Cats

Do not attempt to groom the following cats:

phantom cats
psychic cats
any of Grimalkin's offspring

Most Uber cats are okay with your touching them; do so at your own risk.

Dragons

Okay to groom the following as instructed:

Celtic dragons - scissors

Northern Baltic dragons - rocks

Puff, the Magic Dragon –paper

– Marge Simon

TRAINING

Uber Cats: Need no training

Dragons:

LIE DOWN: This needs be taught before flight training. Using a dragon dummy, gently lower it to a prone position. Then pretend to get on it. This has worked in 1 out of 10,000 cases, but stick with it. Sooner or later, the dragon will get the connection.

FLY: Actually, you need not teach a winged dragon to fly, but you might want to train it to carry yourself or groceries. Best to start at an early age, such as 50 or 100 years.

FETCH: Dragons do not fetch willingly, unless it is something that belongs to them, such as its treasure, for relocation purposes.

SIT: One of the easier commands. Most dragons are vain and love to have their photograph taken or their portrait painted.

ROLL OVER: Useful for preparing ground for a garden or a picnic. Demonstrate the action of rolling over using a dragon dummy. Do not roll on the ground yourself, or you may well be rolled upon and squished.

Miscellany: Use of cell phones.

Uber cats: Most breeds will not tolerate bells, buzzers or incoming call alerts. Some have been known to carry a phone into the bathroom and drop it in the crapper.

Dragons: Many species enjoy the easy convenience of chatting with others while flying or in meetings with other dragons. This does not apply to dates with virgins.

– Marge Simon

Never Text a Dragon When He's Down

Once I owned the finest dragon in the land.
He took first place at dragon shows and then –
his mate left him for another,
he got a message from her brother,
oh, never text a dragon when he's down.

Chorus:

Never text a dragon when he's down,
it may seem elementary,
when he's so complementary
BUT!
never text a dragon when he's down.

My friends I swear to you this tale is true,
my favorite was a dragon gold and blue,
he got his own cell phone,
told me "UR on UR own",
oh, never text a dragon when he's down.

Never text a dragon when he's down,
it may seem elementary,
when he's so complementary
BUT!
never text a dragon when he's down.

– *Marge Simon*

Evil Dragon-Flies

Sometimes one of them gets inside and soars around the kitchen. That makes the Female nervous, because she's afraid of them. I've seen my Master's hand grab the air as fast as I can run. Then he goes outside and comes back looking proud. He never misses.

I don't know why he keeps returning them outside. But that's the way of things around here.

The Female is Master's fifth cousin once removed, whatever that means. Master's relatives sent her to live with us when Master's momma died. I thought she was plain stupid. She swatted one of them when Master wasn't around. It fell on the floor by my food bowl.

I shouldn't have eaten it. I hadn't been hungry in the first place, but when it moved, I couldn't help myself.

The Female screamed and Master came running. Next thing I know, he grabs my tail and hangs me upside down. He kept me like that until it came swooshing out of my mouth, wet and highly pissed.

"It's bad riled," Master said. "I can't touch it right now. You best git, Cat."

So I hid under the porch until dark, hoping it would forget once it dried out. They have a short attention span. I forget where I heard that, but probably it was Master. He's always hanging around in the kitchen after dinner like I do. Only not for the same reason. It's because he likes to watch that Female do the cleaning up.

I figured he was back with her by the time I crawled out. I was wrong. He was sitting on the porch step.

"Mind now," he said, " it's still in the kitchen somewhere. Stay away from there until tomorrow." He dusted off his pants. "Got chores."

I've never been good at following advice. Not even from Master, so I went straight back there. I felt it hit the back of my neck with its stinger and next thing, the Female's voice was calling my name. I hit the floor and passed out.

When I came about, Master told me what happened. I was amazed. The Female looks too weak to lift a cast iron pot, much less move fast enough to capture one under the lid. As soon as I could walk, I started by rubbing her legs. I forgot how sharp my whiskers are until I saw the scratches. She smiled and patted my nose. Then she poured cream in my bowl.

I guess she'll do. Long as I keep her on her toes.

– *Marge Simon*

My Pointy Hat

I was born with a pointy head. The aunties laughed it off. They
weren't expecting me to stay that way. When I was five, I jumped
off the roof of the garage. I thought I could fly, but I merely sailed
through the air and landed on my pointy head.

After that they spoke in hushed voices whenever I came near. The
next nine years were difficult.
Many of them I spent waiting at the top of the stairs when company
came, hoping someone would notice me. Everyone had a special

talent. Uncle Rem had twenty fingers. He juggled all sorts of things, living or dead. Grandma Mattie communed with Socrates. All the cousins could levitate with ease. Great Uncle Ivan was usually late. He'd teleport in at the last minute. I may as well have been invisible. So I stayed in my room and played with my pets.

I found the first in winter, when it was snowing really hard. A couple of baby frost dragons dropped out of the sky. They flopped around making sad squawky sounds. I hunkered down and talked to them inside my head. They'd told me they'd been lost during a migration. So I reduced them and they flapped into my pocket.

On a walk deep in the forest, I heard a creature calling to me outside an evil hag's hut. It was just born, and its mother had abandoned it. It looked like a little kitten but it wasn't, exactly. A grimalkin had gotten amorous with the neighbor's cat, and – well, I couldn't just leave it there. So again, into my pocket it went.

The day I turned fifteen I was summoned to the parlor.

Auntie Orange spoke first. "It's time you knew."

"Yes, and it's past time as far as I'm concerned," said Auntie Blue.

"Knew what? That I'm different?" I said.

"You'll never fly. For all we know you're as common as a bean," said Auntie Mauve, wiping her nose delicately with a handkerchief.

Auntie Orange looked distressed. "Well, we really don't know what to do about you. Your parents refused to keep you. We'd assumed it was because of your...affliction."

My neck felt hot. "I suppose you think I owe you?"

"Not at all, dear," said Auntie Blue. "We're giving you another chance. If you can't fly, there might be something else you can do." She frowned at Auntie Mauve.

I rolled my eyes. Then I went to my room and put a change of clothes in a duffle bag. I was about to walk out when I realized I couldn't leave my pets here. So I stuck them in my shirt pocket.

"What are you doing with them?" Auntie Mauve was standing in the door, arms folded.

"Nothing. They're mine, is all. Got them downsized for transport. I trained them."

"What kind of pets are they?"

"Well, there's the dragons; I've taught them to fetch shiny stuff. A kitten abandoned by a witch's familiar – she's really good at making things disappear on command. And a snail. I call him Euclid. He doesn't do anything much, but I really like him and – "

"You say you trained them?" Auntie Mauve stepped closer to peer into my pocket. She sucked in her breath and clicked her tongue. Next thing I knew, her boney arms were wrapped around me so hard I couldn't breathe.

She led me down to the parlor, a smile on her face. "Sisters, I've changed my mind."

I showed them what my pets could do. Auntie Blue gave me a hat so large it came down to my ears. I think this means the next time when company comes, I get to stay downstairs.

– *Marge Simon*

BREEDING

Uber cats: It is unadvisable to direct romantic coupling without the advice of someone steeped in arcane knowledge such as a warlock or demon with doctorates in the subject.

Dragons: Female dragons will let you know when they are ready to mate. Males can sense females in heat all over the globe, so there's nothing you need to do other than get out of his way.

– Marge Simon

DISCIPLINE

Discipline such as humans think of it is not advisable with either Uber Cats or Dragons of any sort; they have their own ways of self-discipline.

Streets of Toledo (The Dragon's Song)

As I walked out in the streets of Toledo
As I walked out in Toledo one day,
I spied a bold dragon wrapped up in white linen
All wrapped in white linen and pale as the clay.

"I see by your outfit that you are a human,"
These words he did say as I tried to slip by,
"Come sit here beside me and hear my sad story
I've done a misdeed and I know I might cry."

'Twas once with my owner I used to go walking'
Once in with my owner I used to go gay,
He lead to me to drinkin', and then to the gamblin',
I'm down in the crest and I'm mournful today."

"Oh, pray you must tell me now where is your owner
and pray tell me true did you lose all his dough?
Can you be feeling guilty and that's what's the matter?
Otherwise why be talking and crying all so?"

"Tis true I did gamble all day in the bar room,
Tis true I got drunk, that I cannot deny,
Soon forgot where I was and I sat on my owner,
he's in hospital now and I fear he might die."

"Let six handsome matrons come serve me a supper,
Let six pretty virgins pour red wine in my grail,
Throw bunches of roses all over my great wings,
Throw roses to lighten my heart of travail."

"Oh, beat the drum slowly, and play the fife lowly,
And play the dragon march as you carry me along,
Take me to the green valley and lay the gals o'er me
For I'm a poor dragon and I know I've done wrong"

– *Marge Simon*

REWARDING YOUR PET

Rewards You May Or May Not Expect from Your Pet

The authors of this manual concur that this is totally up to the owner. Be advised that careless owners may literally become their pet's reward.

Dragon rewards may include (1.) the carcass of a knight or (2.) his suit of shining armor, with perhaps some morsels of his remains inside, though this is a rarity. Dragons are not known to give their treasure to owners, unless it's a kiddy ring from a gumball machine. Take note: treat such tokens with great respect.

Uber Cats are less predictable. Sometimes they eat their prey and all you get are a few bones, or a unicorn horn, possibly the tip of a very small dragon's tail.

– Marge Simon

ADVICE

Advice from a Dragon

Keep an eye on your hoard.
If somebody contradicts you, eat them.
Knights – they're not just for breakfast anymore.
If somebody asks you for a light, oblige willingly.
Fly high and keep your fangs sharp.

Advice from a Saber Toothed Tiger

Remember to brush and floss.
Remember, you have a very memorable grin.
Extinct? Are you sure?
If something troubles you, rip its throat out.
What happens in the Paleolithic, stays in the Paleolithic.

– Mary Turzillo

RECIPES

Merlin's Muffins *by Monthra Stewart*

Dragons enjoy this treat, straight from Merlin's girlfriend's cookbook.

(makes enough for one medium sized dragon's snack)

sift together:
2 cups flour
1 tsp. baking powder
1/2 tsp. salt

cream:
1 c. brown sugar
1 c. butter

blend in:
one whole beaten to pieces dodo egg, or one chicken egg

Gradually add to dry mixture.
2 Tb. maple syrup or the blood of an ox
If it's too thick, add 1/3 c. water or 1/3 c. merlot

Pour in lined muffin pans and cook at 350 degrees
until about seven after ten, if you put them in at 9:30

Let sit 5 min to rise and calm down. Serve warm.

– Marge Simon

Zanzibar Zinnia Pudding *by Granny Retch*

Since even cats of mythic origin like to nibble on plants, here's a dessert that should please even the most particular feline's fancy for flowers.

2 cups zinnia petals of any color
30 hummingbird eggs or 2 hen's eggs
2 cups milk of a Zanzibar (or milk of a cow, but not milk of magnesia)
1/2 cup beet, cane, raw, rare, medium, or well-done sugar
1 Tb. butter
a few drops of catnip or mint extract

Soak the zinnia petals in the milk for one hour, strain out petals, and put milk in the top of a double boiler over simmering water. Add sugar and allow it to dissolve.

Beat the eggs until they scream or become thick and yellow. Add some of the milk to the eggs, beating constantly, and then pour that mixture into the milk in the double boiler, being careful to not let the eggs curdle from pouring them into the hot milk too quickly. If they do curdle, don't worry as most cats don't really care if their pudding is lumpy or not...except for cats from Zanzibar who expect perfection and will devour you if the pudding isn't smooth and lump-free.

Stir constantly until pudding thickens. Once it has, remove the top of the double boiler from the heat, stir in the extract, pour into serving-sized pet bowls, and allow to cool.

Don't be upset if your feline decides to roll in it instead of eating it. Pick out the stray fur, refrigerate what's left, and serve it to whichever relative you dislike the most.

– Ree Young

63

Thai Roasted Maiden *by Granny Retch*

This is an old recipe that is fondly remembered by dragons of advanced years. In ancient times, roasted maidens were easy enough to come by; however, nowadays, that sort of thing is frowned upon, plus maidens are in scarcer supply. Chicken is substituted now; it tastes a lot like maiden, anyway.

1 large whole chicken (or small maiden)
1 handful each of rosemary, parsley, thyme, and sage
salt and pepper to taste
Clean out the inside of the chicken/maiden and save the giblets and such for gravy.
Place the handfuls of herbs inside the chicken/maiden cavity, but be sure to remove the claws/hands. Sprinkle the cavity with salt and pepper.

Place in a roasting pan and bake for 1 hour at 325 degrees or for 2 minutes if your dragon is the fire-breathing variety and uses that skill to cook the "body" at 2,900 degrees. If using your dragon's fiery breath, be sure to cook "body" in a metal pan as glass will melt at that temperature, hardening later as the "body" cools, making it too crunchy for a dragon's taste. They prefer tender meat, which is why tender maidens have been such a popular main dish.

Take the saved innards, place in pot with water to cover, and simmer till cooked through. Strain out the innards. Use the liquid for gravy by adding cornstarch to some cold water, mixing that well, and pouring it into the hot liquid, stirring vigorously the whole time. Add salt and pepper to taste. Place the innards just outside your dragon's lair to lure a carnivorous animal or two for your dragon's midnight snack.

Place the gravy in a bowl for your dragon to lap up since it will no doubt eat the roasted chicken or maiden in one gulp before you can ladle any gravy on it.

Serves one tiny dragon, appeases a small dragon as a snack, and barely makes a dent in a large dragon's appetite.
– *Ree Young*

Chilled Dragon Egg Magical Cat Tail Soup

There are dozens of recipes for magical green cat-tail-dragon egg soup on the web. Some use cream or salt or olive oil. I like a simpler, less heavy version. My resident knight in silicon armor really liked this.
Put in blender the following:

1 and 1/2 or 2 ripe dragon eggs (discard the central pit and scaly peel, silly)
 about six inches of an unpeeled magical green cat-tail
1 cup vegetable broth
1 cup low-fat yoghurt or kefir (you could use buttermilk)
1 T chopped onion
1 T chopped fresh mint (maybe parsley would work if the fresh mint in your garden has been destroyed by magical green cats looking for catnip)
1 T lemon juice (might try lime for extra zip)
1 T rice vinegar (I happened to have rice vinegar, but you could probably use a half T of white vinegar, or more lemon juice. Apple vinegar might spoil the color.)

Blend the hell out of it. Make sure you get all the lumps out.
Chill it for at least four hours to chill any residual embryonic dragon fire.
Place in pretty bowls and garnish. (I used a dollop of Greek yoghurt, a sprig of mint, and a nasturtium blossom)

I forgot to mention: For the dragon egg, you can substitute an avocado. And if you are unable to catch a magical green cat and deprive it of its tail (they do regenerate, just like iguana tails, incidentally, although the magical green cat will be very annoyed and possibly claw your eyes out), use an English cucumber.

— *Mary Turzillo*

Marge Simon free lances as a writer-poet-illustrator for genre and mainstream publications such as *Strange Horizons, Niteblade, DailySF Magazine, Pedestal, Dreams & Nightmares*. She edits a column for the *HWA Newsletter*, "Blood & Spades: Poets of the Dark Side." She won the *Strange Horizons* Best Poem Award, 2010. In addition to her poetry, she has published two prose collections: *Christina's World*, Sam's Dot Publications, 2008 and *Like Birds in the Rain*, Sam's Dot, 2007. She won the Bram Stoker for Best Poetry Collection with Charlie Jacob, *Vectors: A Week in the Death of a Planet*, Dark Regions Press, 2008. New poetry collections in 2011: *Unearthly Delights* (self-illustrated in color, Sam's Dot Publications), *The Mad Hattery* (illustrated by Sandy DeLuca, Electrikmilkbath Press). www.margesimon.com

Mary A. Turzillo's novel *An Old-Fashioned Martian Girl* and Nebula-Award-winning novelette "Mars Is no Place for Children" are recommended reading on the International Space Station. She has been nominated for the Rhysling, the British Science Fiction Association Award ("Eat or Be Eaten, a Love Story"), and the Pushcart *(Your Cat & Other Space Aliens*, vanZeno). She has recent and forthcoming work in *Asimov's, Paper Crow, Analog, New Myths, Strange Horizons, Bull Spec, Magazine of Speculative Poetry, Ladies of Trade Town*, and *Stone Telling*, plus an authorized Philip José Farmer sequel story, "The Beast Erect," in *The Worlds of Philip José Farmer 2*, Meteor Press, 2011.

www.ingramcontent.com/pod-product-compliance
Lightning Source LLC
Chambersburg PA
CBHW070808120626
46557CB00002B/769